nipêhon

—

ᓂ ᐧᐁᐦᐅᐣ

—

I Wait

Caitlin Dale Nicholson
asici / ᐊᓯᒋ / with
Leona Morin-Neilson

GROUNDWOOD BOOKS
HOUSE OF ANANSI PRESS
Toronto   Berkeley

nôhkom mamanêw.   ᓄᐦᑯᑦ ᒪᒪᓇᐤ   Nôhkom gets ready.

nipêhon.   σ∨ᶫᐅᐤᵡ   I wait.

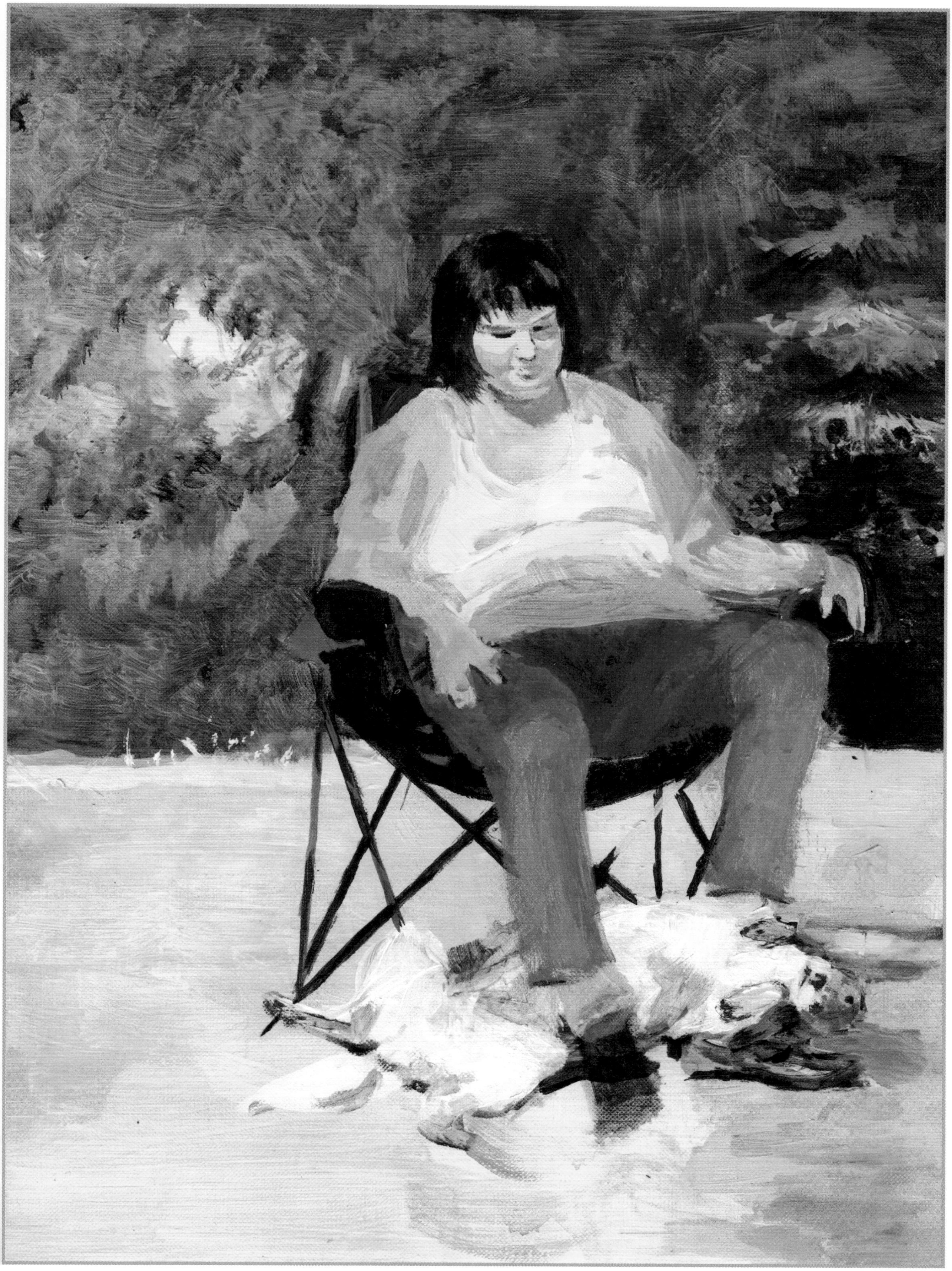

nikâwiy pêhow. σᑳᐃᐧᐩ ᐯᐦᐅᐤ᙮ Mom waits.

nôhkom pimohtêw.　　ᓄᐦᑯᒼ ᐱᒧᐦᑌᐤ×　　Nôhkom walks.

nipimohtân.  I walk.

nikâwiy pimohtêw.   ᓂᑲᐄᐧᐟ ᐱᒧᐦᑌᐤˣ   Mom walks.

nôhkom ayamihâw.   ᓄᐦᑯᑦ ᐊᔭᒥᐦᐋᐤ.   Nôhkom prays.

nitayamihân. ᓂᑕᔭᒥᐦᐋᐣ. I pray.

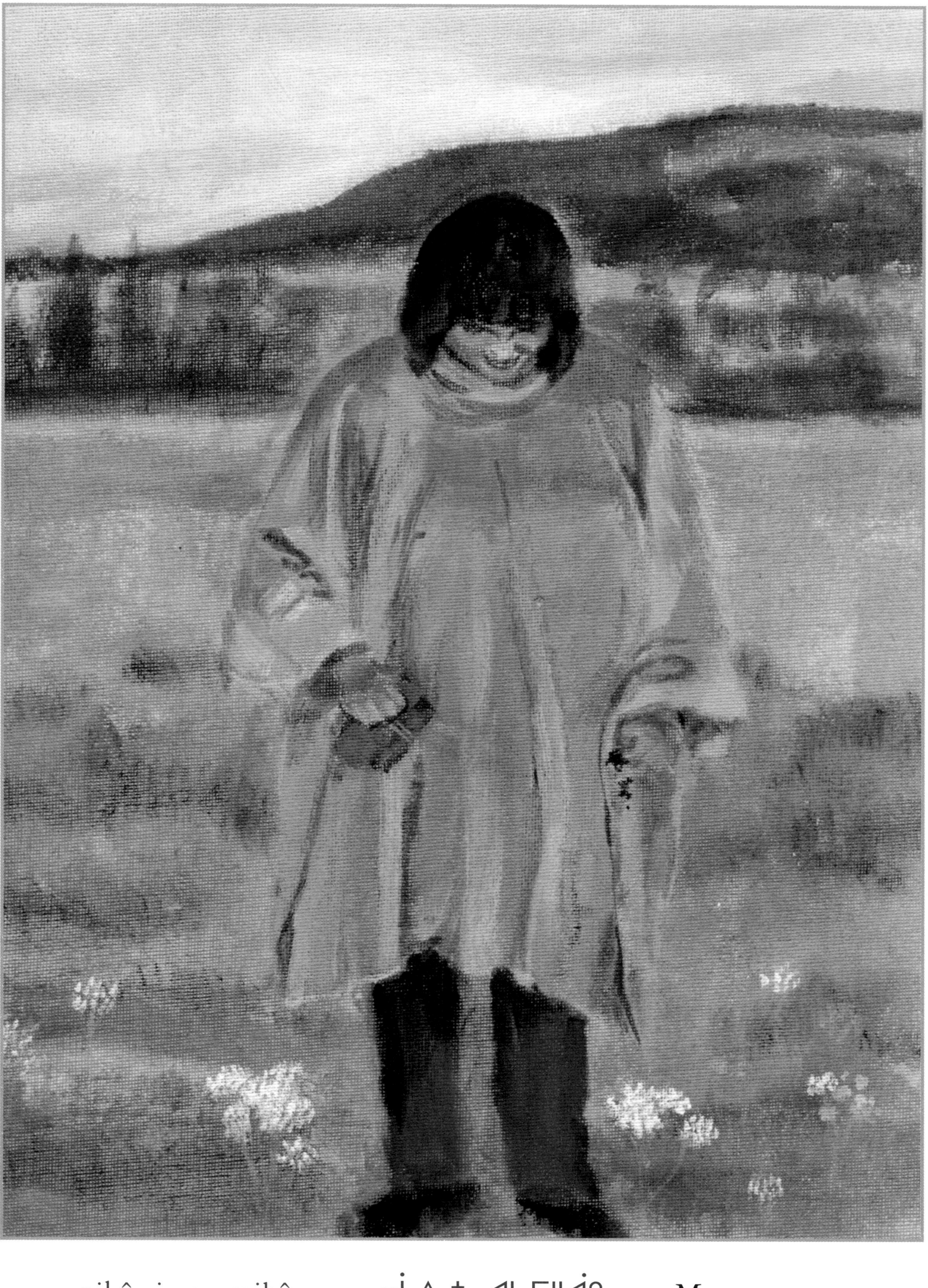

nikâwiy ayamihâw. ᓂᑳᐃᐧᐩ ᐊᔭᒥᐦᐋᐤ᙮ Mom prays.

nôhkom môsâhkinam.   ᓄᐦᑯᒼ ᒨᓵᐦᑭᓇᒼ᙮   Nôhkom picks.

nimôsâhkinên.   ᓂ ᒨᓵᐦᑭᓀᐣ×   I pick.

nikâwiy mâka?   σbΔ·+ Ḃb?   **Mom?**

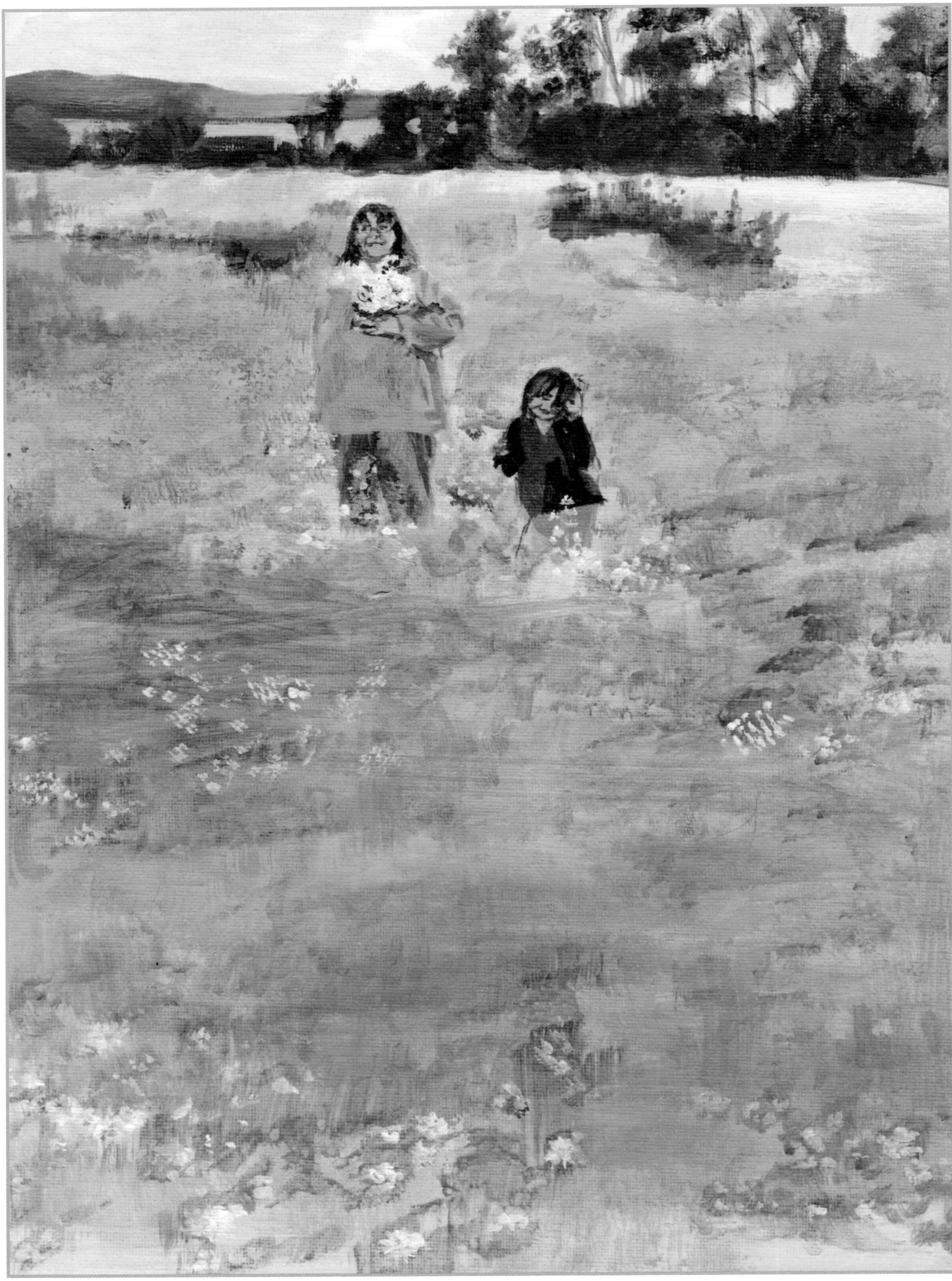

niyanân nipêhonân. ᓂᑳᐃᐧᐩ ᒨᓵᐦᑭᓇᐨ᙮ We wait.

nikâwiy môsâhkinam.   ᓂᑲᐄᐧ ᒨᓵᐦᑭᓇᒼ   Mom picks.

nôhkom kîsihtâw.   ᓄᐦᑯᒼ ᑮᓯᐦᑖᐤ.   Nôhkom is done.

nikîsihtânân!   ᓂᑭᓯᐦᑖᓈᐣ!   We are done!

wâpanêwask nihtiy

ᐧᐄᐸᓄᐊᐧᐧᑎ ᓂᐦᑎ

nêwo minihkwâcikana nipiy
nêwo êmihkwânisak wâpanêwask wâpikwaniya,
  oski-nîpiya ahpô ê-pâstêki.

kisâkamisa nipiy; ohtêki, êkota wâpanêwask
  ka-takonên.
pêho niyânan cipahikanisa, sîkopwâtina êkwa
  minihkwê.
kika-kî-minihkwân ê-kisâkamitêk ahpô
  ê-tahkâkamik — ê-kisâkamitêyik
  ka-miyoskâkow awiyak ê-kisisot.

ᓄᐅᐧ ᒥᓂᐦᒃᐧᐄᒋᑲᓇ ᓂᐱᔨ
ᓄᐅᐧ ᐁᒥᐦᒃᐧᐊᓂᐢ ᐧᐄᐸᓄᐊᐧᐧᑎ ᐧᐄᐱᒃᐧᓂᐢ,
  ᐅᐢᑭ ᓅᐱᐧ ᐊᐦᐳᐧ ᐁ ᐧᐊᐢᑌᑭᕁ

ᑭᐢᐊᑲᒥᐢ ᓂᐱᔨ; ᐅᐦᑌᑭ, ᐁᑯᑕ ᐧᐄᐸᓄᐊᐧᐧᑎ
  ᑲ ᑕᑯᓄᕁ
ᐯᐦᐅ ᓂᐧᐋᓇᐤ ᒥᐸᐦᐄᑲᓂᐢ, ᓯᑯ ᐧᐊᑎᓇ ᐁᑯᐧ ᒥᓂᐦᑫᕁ
ᑭᑲ ᑮ ᒥᓂᐦᒃᐧ ᐁ ᑭᐢᐊᒥᑌᐢ ᐊᐦᐳᐧ ᐁ ᑕᐦᑲᒥᐢ —
  ᐁ ᑭᐢᐊᒥᑌᐢ ᑲ ᒥᔪᐢᑲᑯᐤ ᐊᐃᐧᐧᐢ ᐁ ᑭᓯᓱᕁ

Yarrow Tea

4 cups water
4 tablespoons yarrow flowers and leaves, fresh
  or dried

Bring water to a boil, then add yarrow.
Steep for five minutes, strain and enjoy.
Drink hot or cold — hot to relieve a fever.

ninanâskomâwak kahkiyaw aniki iskwêwak mîna iskwêsisak kâ-kî-pê-kiskêyimakik
êkwa mîna mistahi kihci-kîkway kâ-kî-kiskinwahamawicik. tâhto-kîsikâw kêyâpic *Leona*,
Maria êkwa *Avery* niwâpahtahikwak iyikohk ê-kihcêyihtâkwahk nôtokwêwak, iskwêwak
êkwa oskinîkiskwêwak ka-mâmawohkamâtocik kahkiyaw kîkway. ôta masinahikanihk
wâpahcikâtêwa êkoni ôhi kâ-mâh-miyitocik: kiskêyihtamowin, sîpiyawêsiwin,
sawêyimitowin êkwa môcikihtâwin. êwako anima nîsta tahto-askiy ê-kî-pê-miyicik.

Caitlin

ôma masinahikan nitosîhtamawâw *Avery* – kâkikê niya wiya, Sîkwan Maskwa ôma kiya.
kîstawâw mîna nitânisak *Maria* mîna *Lori*, nôsisimak *Austin* mîna *Gabriel*, êkwa mîna
ninâpêm *John*, kinanâskomitinâwâw ê-wîcihiyêk ê-sîtoskawiyêk êkwa ê-sîhkimiyêk
ê-mâwasakonamahk maskihkiya ta-piponi-nihtîhkêyahk.

kisâkihitinâwâw,
Leona
kôhkom, kikâwiy, kiwîkimâkan

σαἀᶮᴰᴸ⊲˙ᐦ ᖯᴵᴵᴾᐳᵒ ⊲ᶳᴾ ∆ᶇᑫ˙⊲˙ᐦ ᖸᥑ ∆ᶇᑫ˙ᣝᐦ ᖯ ᖭ Ⅴ ᑭᶇᑫ᠊ᐳᴸᴾᐦ
∇ᖯ˙ ᖸᥑ ᖸᐣᑕᴵᴵ∆ ᑭᴵᴵᖸ ᖭᖯ˙⁺ ᖯ ᖭ ᑭᐣᑫᥑ᠊ᴵᴵ⊲ᴸ∆˙ᶈᐤ ᐤᴵᴵᐧ ᖮᖷᖯᵒ ᑫᖯᐱ᠆
Leona, Maria ∇ᖯ˙ *Avery* σᐧᐧ᠊ᐸᴵᴵᑕᴵᴵ∆ᖯ˙ᐦ ∆ᐳᗢᶍ ∇ ᑭᴵᴵᒉᐳᴵᴵᖮ᠋ᖯ˙ᶍ ᖷᐣᑫ˙⊲˙ᐦ,
∆ᶇᑫ˙⊲˙ᐦ ∇ᖯ˙ ᐤᐣᑭᖮᶈᶇᑫ˙⊲˙ᐦ ᖯ ᒡᒡᐤᐧᴵᴵᖯᒡᐤ᠋ᐦ ᖯᴵᴵᴾᐳᵒ ᖭᖯ˙⁺ᣝ ᐤᑕ
ᒷᥑᴵᴵ∆ᖯᶍ ᐧᐧ᠊ᐸᴵᴵᖸᖯᑌ⊲˙ ∇ᖁᶳ ᐤᴵᴵ∆ ᖯ ᒷᴵᴵ ᖸᐳᒡᖸᐦ : ᑭᶇᑫᐳᴵᴵᖮᒡ∆˙ᐳ,
ᖭ᠋ᐳ∇˙ᣝ∆˙ᐳ, ᐢ∇᠊ᐳᖸᒡ∆˙ᐳ ∇ᖯ˙ ᒷᣝᴾᴵᴵᒉ∆˙ᐳᣝ ∇⊲ᒡ ⊲ᶳᒷ ᖮᶇᑕ
ᑕᴵᴵᒡ ⊲ᐣᴾ⁺ ∇ ᖭ Ⅴ ᖸᐳᖸᐦᣝ

Caitlin

ᐤᒷ ᒷᥑᴵᴵ∆ᖯᐳ σᒡᖭ᠋ᴵᴵᒉᒷᐧ˙ᵒ *Avery* – ᖯᖁᑫ σᐳ ∆᠊ᐳ, ᖭ᠋ᖯᐧ ᒷᖯ˙ ᐤᒷ ᖭᐳᣝ
ᖭᐣᑕᐧ˙ᵒ ᖸᥑ σᒉᶳᐦᐦ *Maria* ᖸᥑ Lori, ᐤ᠋ᣝᣝᒷᐦ *Austin* ᖸᥑ *Gabriel*,
∇ᖯ˙ ᖸᥑ σᒉᐧ˙ᐅᶜ *John*, ᖯᒷᐧᶮᒡᖸᖮᒷᐧ˙ᵒ ∇ ᐧ˙᠊ᴵᴵ∆ᐦᐦ ∇ ᖭ᠋ᒡᶇᖯ∆˙ᐦᐦ
∇ᖯ˙ ∇ ᖭ᠋ᴵᴵᴾᖸᐦᐦ ∇ ᒷ⊲᠊ᐢᒡᐤᒷᶍ ᒷᐣᴾᴵᴵᴾᐳ ᒡ ᐳᐳσ σᴵᴵᖷᴵᴵᑫᐳᶍᣝ

ᖭ᠋ᖯᴾᴵᴵ∆ᖸᒷᐧ˙ᵒ,
Leona
ᖑᴵᴵᒡᶜ, ᑭᖯ∆˙⁺, ᖭᐧ˙᠊ᖭᒷᖯᐳ

I'd like to dedicate this book to the women and girls who have passed through my life
and taught me many valuable lessons. Leona, Maria and Avery show me every day the
importance of different generations of women working together and connecting. This
book reflects the knowledge, the patience, the love and the fun they share with each
other and have shared with me throughout the years.

Caitlin

This book is dedicated to Avery — you will always be my Spring Bear.
For my daughters Maria and Lori, my grandsons Austin and Gabriel, and my husband
John, for your help, support and encouragement for picking herbs for the winter teas.

Love,
Leona
Grandmother, Mother, Wife

nanâskomowina

namôya ôma masinahikan kita-kî-ihkin kîspin êkâ ê-sîtoskâkoyahkok kinâpêminawak,
ê-atoskêcik askîhk, êkosi kiyânaw iskwêwak ka-kaskihtâyahk ka-mâwasakonamahk
nanâtohk iyinito-maskihkiya. mistahi ninanâskomimânâna *Leona* onâpêma, iyikohk
ê-kî-pê-sîtoskâkoyâhk tahto-askiy, êkwa mîna ôsisima *Austin* êkwa *Gabriel*.
kinanâskomitinân *Dalton*, *Garth* êkwa *Oscar*, iyikohk ê-kî-sîhkimiyâhk mîna
ê-kî-sîtoskawiyâhk. *BC Arts Council*, kinanâskomitinâwâw sôniyâw kâ-kî-miyiyêk
ka-mâcihtâyân ôma masinahikan, êkwa mîna *Antonia* êkwa *Dee* ê-kî-mamihcimiyêk
ta-wîcihiyêk ispîhk sôniyâw kâ-kî-nitotamâkêyân. ispîhk tahtwâw
kâ-mâh-masinahikêyân, nikâwîs *Juanita*, tâpitawi kikî-mâmitonêyimitin.
tâpwê piko kiya ohci nikî-nôhtê-kîsihtân.

ᓇᐋᐣᑯᒧᐤᐃᐧᐊ

ᓇᒫᐟ ᐅᒪ ᒪᓯᓇᐦᐃᐠᐟ ᑭᑕ ᐦ ᐃᐦᑭ ᑭᓅᐱ ᐁᐧᑳ ᐁ ᐦᑐᐣᑳᐦᐧᐨᒹᐨ ᑭᐋᐯᒥᓇᐊᐧᐢ,
ᐁ ᐊᐟᐣᑀᐢ ᐊᐧᐦᐢᐢ, ᐁᐧᐢᐧ ᑭᐧᐊᐤ ᐃᐢᐧᐁᐊᐧᐢ ᐦ ᑲᐢᑭᐦᑖᔭᐢ ᐦ ᐧᒳᐢᐧᑯᓇᒪᐢ ᓇᐋᐣᑐᐦᐠ
ᐃᔨᓂᐟ ᒪᐢᑭᐦᐠᔭ Leona ᐅᐋᐯᒪ, ᐃᔨᑯᐦᐠ ᐁ ᑭ ᐯ ᐦᑐᐣᐧᑳᐧᐢᐤ
ᑖᐦᑐ ᐊᐢᑮ, ᐁᐧᐤ ᒫ ᐅᐧᐢᒥᒪ Austin ᐁᐧᐤ Gabriel×. ᑭᓇᐋᐣᑯᒥᑎᐋᐣ Dalton,
Garth ᐁᐧᐤ Oscar, ᐃᔨᑯᐦᐠ ᐁ ᑭ ᐦᐧᐁᑯᒥᔭᐦᐠ ᒫ ᐁ ᑭ ᐦᐟᐣᐧᑯᐦᐧᔭᐦᐠ×. BC Arts Council,
ᑭᓇᐋᐣᑯᒥᑎᓇᐊᐧᐤ ᐦᓄᔭᐤ ᐦ ᑭ ᒥᔦᐢ ᐦ ᒫᐦᐨᑖᔭᐤ ᐅᒪ ᒪᓯᓇᐦᐃᐠᐟ, ᐁᐧᐤ ᒫ
Antonia ᐁᐧᐤ Dee ᐁ ᑭ ᒪᒥᐦᐨᒥᔭᐢ ᑕ ᐧᐄᐦᐨᐦᐃᔭᐢ ᐊᐣᐧᐊᐢ ᐦᓄᔭᐤ ᐦ ᑭ ᓄᐟᐟᒫᑫᔭᐢ×.
ᐃᐢᐧᐊᐢ ᑖᐦᐧᒳ ᐦ ᒫᐢ ᒪᓯᓇᐦᐃᑫᔭᐢ, ᓄᑳᐧᐄᐣ Juanita, ᒑᐟᒑᐧ ᑭᑭ ᒫᒧᑐᐋᐢᑎᐣᐟ×.
ᒑᐯ ᐱᑯ ᑭᔭ ᐅᐦᐨ ᓂᑭ ᓅᐦᐟ ᑮᐢᐦᐟ×.

Acknowledgments

This book wouldn't be possible without the men in our lives who help us on the land so we
can do what women need to do to gather medicines for their families. Many thanks go out to
Leona's husband, John, for all his help through the years, and grandsons, Austin and Gabriel.
Thanks to Dalton and Garth and Oscar for the encouragement and support. Thank you to the
BC Arts Council for giving me a grant to start the book, and to Antonia and Dee for giving
me glowing references for the grant application. Aunt Juanita, you were always on my mind as
I put each page together. I needed to finish for you.

Note
This book is written in Cree (the Y dialect) and English. The
Cree language is represented in two forms — standard roman
orthography and syllabics. *nôhkom* is Cree for "my grandmother,"
but *kôhkom*, "your grandmother," is the form that has been
borrowed into English and is now used generically for "Grandma."
In the Cree and Tahltan cultures, and in many other aboriginal
nations, children have many *kôhkoms*. Young people today use
kôhkom as a term of love and respect for women elders.

The publisher would like to thank Dr. Arok Wolvengrey and Dr.
Jean Okimâsis of First Nations University of Canada for editing
and providing syllabics for the Cree text.

Text and illustrations copyright © 2017 by Caitlin Dale Nicholson
Published in Canada and the USA in 2017 by Groundwood Books

Groundwood Books / House of Anansi Press
groundwoodbooks.com

We acknowledge for their financial support of our publishing
program the Canada Council for the Arts, the Ontario Arts Council
and the Government of Canada.

Library and Archives Canada Cataloguing in Publication
Nicholson, Caitlin Dale, author
    Nipêhon = I wait / Caitlin Dale Nicholson, Leona
Morin-Neilson.

Issued in print and electronic formats.
Text in Cree (romanized and syllabic characters) and English.
ISBN 978-1-55498-914-0 (hardcover). —
ISBN 978-1-55498-915-7 (PDF)

    I. Morin-Neilson, Leona, author II. Nicholson, Caitlin Dale.
I wait. III. Nicholson, Caitlin Dale. I wait. Cree. IV. Title.
V. Title: I wait.

PS8627.I239N56 2017   jC813'.6   C2016-908273-3
C2016-908274-1

The illustrations were done in acrylics.
Design by Michael Solomon
Printed and bound in Malaysia

FSC
www.fsc.org
MIX
Paper from
responsible sources
FSC® C012700

Canada Council   Conseil des Arts
for the Arts   du Canada

ONTARIO ARTS COUNCIL
CONSEIL DES ARTS DE L'ONTARIO
an Ontario government agency
un organisme du gouvernement de l'Ontario

With the participation of the Government of Canada
Avec la participation du gouvernement du Canada | Canadä